W9-AXE-493

The Best Horse Ever

By **Alice DeLaCroix**

Illustrated by
Ron Himler

Holiday House / New York

Text copyright © 2010 by Alice DeLaCroix
Illustrations copyright © 2010 by Ron Himler
All Rights Reserved
Holiday House is registered in the U.S. Patent and Trademark Office.
Printed and Bound in January 2010 at Maple Vail, Binghamton, NY, USA.
www.holidayhouse.com
First Edition
1   3   5   7   9   10   8   6   4   2

Library of Congress Cataloging-in-Publication Data
DeLaCroix, Alice.
The best horse ever / by Alice DeLaCroix ; illustrated by
Ronald Himler. — 1st ed.
p. cm.
Summary: Nine-year-old Abby finally gets her own horse
but will this new responsibility mean she must give up
everything else?
ISBN 978-0-8234-2254-8 (hardcover)
[1. Horses—Fiction.   2. Responsibility—Fiction.   3. Friendship—Fiction.]
I. Himler, Ronald, ill.   II. Title.
PZ7.D36965Be 2010
[Fic]—dc22
2009025542

To my husband Bob—
simply the best

Contents

Chapter 1

The Greatest Horse Ever

Abby flew into the house. She had the best, the most exciting can't-wait news ever. The best news of the whole summer. Of her whole life!

"Mom, Dad!" She slid into her chair at the kitchen table. "My horse—"

"Wash your hands, Abby," said Mom.

Hands. Washing. Not important. Not now! "I washed," Abby said. Well, she *had* a few hours ago.

"Did not," her brother, Brad, said.

"Brat," replied Abby.

"Brad," corrected her father.

"Wash," Mom said.

How could she wait another minute? But Abby darted to the sink and doused her hands. A quick wipe on her jeans and she was back in her chair.

Abby shoved her thick brown hair from her sweaty forehead and took a big breath. Now she could tell what she'd just heard at Blue Ribbon Stables!

But Brad started right up. "You don't have a horse. *We* have a pony."

Abby gritted her teeth. Brad was only seven, two years younger than Abby. Still, he liked to think he knew everything.

"Good old Marshmallow," Dad said with a dopey grin on his face. "You kids learned how to ride on him." Dad had owned Marshmallow a long time.

Abby thought, Yeah—old, tubby, slow Marshmallow. He would never be any taller. She had already outgrown the Welsh pony.

"My horse is for sale!" she blurted before anyone else could stick their ideas in. "Mr. Winkler will sell him now that he's sixteen. Griffin is the greatest lesson horse ever. Probably the greatest *horse* ever—"

Brad butted in. "Except for the Black Stallion and Seabiscuit. Oh, and don't forget Secretariat."

Abby gave him the cold fisheye. She said to her parents, "Griffin is my favorite, favorite, favorite horse, and Mr. Winkler wants to sell him and buy a new younger lesson horse."

Mom said in her calm voice, "You ride well on him, honey."

Abby nodded. "And I love him!"

Brad clutched his chest where his heart was and rolled his eyes heavenward.

Abby aimed an elbow at Brad's side. "And he loves me. I think."

Dad said, "Aah, the course of true love is a rocky one." He grinned.

"You guys," Mom chided. "So what are you saying here, Abby?"

"Well, could we . . . Well, you said . . . Uh . . ." Suddenly words wouldn't come for Abby. It was too, too important.

Dad took pity on her. "We said we could buy you a horse of your own. If the right one showed up at our door."

Abby nodded, beaming. "You did. It did. Almost," she said. "Blue Ribbon Stables is just across the field."

Abby was lucky, she thought. She lived on a farm in pretty western New York. And that farm was right next door to the stable where she took riding lessons, so she could walk to it when she wanted to watch the horses. Today she'd run home from there with her big news.

Mom chewed a bite of salad. She had on her thinking face.

Dad speared a slice of roast beef. Abby watched his tanned cheeks move as he chewed.

Abby wasn't hungry. Her heart beat wildly.

She needed, needed, needed Griffin to be her own horse. It would be perfect.

Brad surprised her by saying, "I wouldn't have to share Marshmallow. Abby and I could ride together."

"You are getting long-legged already, Abby girl," Dad said. "But a horse can be too big to handle. How big is this Griffin?"

"You've seen me ride him, Dad. He's only about fifteen hands tall. And I'm going to keep growing taller." Mom was tall and thin—except for a few bumps here and there—and Abby was sure she would grow up that way, too.

"Which one *is* he?" Dad asked.

"Oh, Mike, you know," said Mom. "You're teasing Abby."

Brad piped up, "He's the bay with a white star."

Abby said, "And he has the longest, fullest black tail."

"And Abby's always hugging him," Brad said.

Abby kept her mouth shut and pushed a pea around her plate. Even fresh homegrown peas that tasted like sugar couldn't tempt her now.

Mom said, "A well-trained lesson horse that's been handled a lot makes a good backyard horse."

Abby knew Mom didn't really mean backyard.

They had a barn with stalls, after all. It just meant a horse you kept at home. Abby was nodding yes as fast as she could. She said, "I know how to take care of him, too."

She went on. "I help with Marshmallow. And at summer camp at the stable, I learned bunches."

Mom rubbed at the spot between her eyebrows where a frown could form. Then she smiled.

Dad scratched his sun-freckled arm. "We'll look into it, Abby," he said.

What did that mean? Abby wondered. Get a magnifying glass? Hire a private detective? Read tea leaves?

She had wanted a YES. But at least she didn't get a big fat NO. "Okay. Okay," she said. Her heartbeat had slowed down to a trot. Maybe, maybe, maybe she'd get her horse.

Chapter 2

Way Better Than Kittens

ooking into it was slow work, in Abby's opinion. She could feel summer vacation running away while her parents made a decision.

Abby took extra pains with helping to care for Marshmallow. "See, Dad. I'm a pro at mucking out a stall. I can even dump the wheelbarrow now, if it's not too full."

Dad nodded. "I've noticed."

She made sure a parent was in hearing distance when she showed Brad how to do a better job of picking out the pony's hooves.

And she wasn't shy about pointing out the super-duper job she'd done keeping the old tack Dad had in good shape.

Mom and Dad had said before that she could have a horse. And Griffin wasn't a fancy young show horse, so Abby was sure money wasn't the problem. Why couldn't they just buy him? Torture!

Almost a week after her big-news day, Abby trudged home in tears. Her mother was crouched clipping marigolds in her flower bed when Abby slunk by.

"Abby?" Mom said. "Abby! What happened? Did you have a fall? I knew I should have picked you up today."

Abby snuffed loudly. "No, I didn't fall off." She hardly *ever* fell off. "I didn't get to ride Griffin."

"Well, honey, that happens lots of times at lessons."

"But, Mo-om," Abby wailed. "Tess—the girl who rode him—was talking to Mr. Winkler. I heard him tell her he already has a buyer for Griffin."

"Oh! Oh, my." Mom dropped her flowers and stood. "We'll have to talk to Mr. Winkler about that. Dad's sure you can handle having a horse. And I'm getting there."

"You're too late already."

"Try not to worry, Abby."

How could she not worry? She knew what she had heard. They were too late.

But, HALLELUJAH! Mom was right. Soon after, everything was settled with Mr. Winkler. Griffin was to be Abby's.

"Yippee!" Abby shouted. She grabbed her parents in a hug. "Thank you, thank you, thank you!" she said. It was perfect.

A couple days later, Abby clutched the phone tightly. "Devon! Can you come over? Now?"

Abby's best friend lived down the road.

"Sure. I'll ask Mom. What's happening?" Devon said.

"Grab your bike and get over here."

"Wait, is your horse coming today? That's it, isn't it? Your horse is—"

"Devon, you goof." Abby frowned. "I told you I get Griffin on Friday. Friday! That's still four whole days from now." Devon spent so much time with her nose in a book or computer, she lost track of the real world. "Are you coming?"

"I'm rolling. Soon," Devon said.

"Soon," Abby answered. She ran down the gravel driveway and watched for the purple bike with the yellow-haired rider speed toward her.

Abby half hopped, half twirled as she waited for Devon. Standing still—not possible. Huh-uh! She was getting Griffin for her very own horse. Sometimes magic really happens, Abby thought.

"So, what is it? What are you so excited about?" Devon asked as soon as she turned off the road.

Abby said, "You'll see. I'll race you to the barn."

"Crazy. I'm on a bike."

Abby took off. "And I've got wings," she called as she ran. She caused Dib and Dab, their two ducks, to squawk and scurry on their wide feet as she flew by.

Devon laughed and didn't pass Abby until they were almost to the barn. She swung off the bike and parked it carefully. "Hey, Tuffy," she said to the little terrier as he ambled out from the barn. "Caught you napping, huh?"

Tuffy put his front feet up on Devon's knees, and she scratched his soft black ears. His straight white tail did its happy-dance. "You are the sweetest dog ever," she said.

"Come on," urged Abby. "You've got to see how the stall looks. You can help me make it perfect." Her brother was always around—even helping sometimes—but Abby needed Devon to be excited about Griffin, too.

"Is that what you called me about?" Devon asked with a twist of her mouth.

Abby was too pumped up to notice. "Yeah! You have to see the stall!"

The barn was tall and painted dark red, as were the other, smaller sheds on the farm. There was a hayloft upstairs, and lots of space, some divided, some open. But for Abby what mattered were the stalls on either side of the center aisle. One stall was Marshmallow's. Across from it was Griffin's. "See," Abby said. "It's bigger than

Marshmallow's. And it has a window so he can look out."

"Uh-huh," agreed Devon. She drifted over to the other stall. "Where's Marshmallow? He's such a cutey."

"Come back, come back. He's outside in the paddock now. But look—see how I swept out all the cobwebs?" Abby pointed to the beams overhead.

Devon looked. "Wow, yeah. Nice." She wrinkled her nose. "Your horse—he's not going to be so big his head would have been in cobwebs way up there, is he?"

Abby set her hands on her hips. "Of course not! He just deserves a really clean house."

Devon nodded. "He's only going to poop in it, you know."

Abby rolled her eyes. "Okay, a clean house to begin with. Don't you help clean your house before company comes so they feel special?"

Devon grinned. "Yeah, but they don't poo—"

"Stop it, you goof," Abby said, and giggled. "Now help me put shavings down on the floor. I want lots and lots of shavings so he has a thick, comfy bed."

Devon laughed. "You sound as if you're getting ready for a baby or something," she said. "Oh,

oh! My cat, Jezebell, is about ready to have her kittens."

"So we'll both be having new animals," Abby said. And secretly she knew her horse was way better than Devon's kittens.

Devon helped Abby pull the big bale of shavings from the storage room into the stall. They opened the bag and started spreading the woody bedding around. She said, "My mom and I put a blanket in a box for Jez, but we don't know if she'll have the kittens there."

"Doesn't this smell good?" Abby asked. "And see, I got a brand-spanking-new feed tub for him."

"Yeah, looks great, Abby." Devon shrugged. "Only, how are you going to have time to play if you're always feeding, cleaning up after, or riding your horse? I got a new computer game."

"Don't be silly, Dev. I'll have plenty of time," Abby said. She felt tight across her shoulders. What was wrong with Devon?

"I better get back home. I want to see whether Jez has her babies yet. Hey, you come too, okay?" Devon was already straddling her bike.

"No thanks. I want to do more here."

"Well, bye. I'll call you if the kitties are born."

Abby nodded. Patting Tuffy's head absent-mindedly, she watched Devon pedal away. She sighed. What could she do now? Everything was ready. If Devon had stayed, they could have found something else to fix up or polish or just pretend about. Why wasn't Devon charged, really charged about Griffin? Abby huffed. Kittens were not exciting. Not one bit.

Chapter 3

Whoa, Griffin

"Why can't I just ride him through the field?" Abby was prancing and a little breathless she was so excited. She wanted to ride Griffin from the stable to her house.

Dad said, "Because Mr. Winkler plans to load Griffin in a trailer and drive over here. All official-like. That's why, Abby girl."

Abby made a face.

"It will be fun," said Mom. "A real event."

And her mother was right. "He's coming!" Abby called. "I can hear the truck. Oh, I can see the horse trailer now." Wow! One of Blue Ribbon Stables' fancy horse trailers coming to her house. Wow!

"Mom! Dad! Come on! He's here, he's here!" Abby called. As the shiny blue trailer pulled into her own driveway, Abby's mouth shut. She could barely breathe. How she'd dreamed of this day, this moment.

Oh, why wasn't Devon here? That would be even more perfect! Abby had told her two o'clock.

But then she heard Griffin whinny, and from the barn Marshmallow answered. Abby laughed out loud.

Mr. Winkler drove past the house and parked near the barn. He was all business while he lowered the back ramp.

Griffin! Abby could see his rich brown flanks, his swishy black tail. The horse stamped his feet.

Brad was at Abby's elbow, silent and wide-eyed for the moment.

Mom had hold of Tuffy's collar, warning the dog to be calm. Tuffy whined and squirmed.

Mr. Winkler entered the trailer from the side door. There he released Griffin's trailer tie, and when he backed him down the loading ramp, Mr. Winkler smiled big as a jack-o'-lantern.

He handed the lead rope over to Abby. "Griffin's all yours now, Abby. Take good care of him."

Abby's head buzzed, and the two words she noticed were "Griffin" and "yours." The best two words in the universe!

"Thank you," she said. She reached up and stroked Griffin's cheek, silky and warm. Was it possible he was really here?

"He's sure nice," Brad said.

Abby nodded, smiling. She looked deep into Griffin's dark brown eyes. He would be smiling too, if horses could, she thought. He was going to be so happy here. With her.

Dad was shaking Mr. Winkler's hand and saying, "Come see where we'll be keeping him."

"Thanks, but I'd better get back. I know Griffin's in a good home."

Dad said, "All right, then. I'll open the stall door for Abby." And he loped into the barn.

Mr. Winkler climbed into his truck and waved good-bye. The engine started with a roar, and off he drove.

Tuffy barked and lunged, then broke from Mom's grasp. His short legs churned after the truck. His sharp yap pierced the air.

"Tuffy!" yelled Mom. She chased the terrier. "Tuffy! You know better." Tuffy kept heading for the road, following the trailer. Mom pounded after him.

Griffin started tossing his head up and down.

"Whoa, whoa, Griffin," Abby said. A lump jumped into her throat.

But the horse was twirling in a circle around her. Abby could barely hold on to the lead rope, he pulled so hard. "Griffin!" Abby shouted. She was afraid he would step on her.

Brad tried to help, but when he grabbed for the rope, he only managed to yank it from Abby's hands.

Griffin spun away from them both. He took off across the barn lot, galloping.

"No-o-o!" screamed Abby. Then she ran after him, tears stinging her eyes. This couldn't be happening. "Griffin," she tried to yell, but a loud *waahh!* blubbed out instead.

The big horse skittered through an open gate and kept right on running.

Chapter 4

Almost Lost

When she reached the gate, Abby had to stop and try to catch her breath.

Dad jogged up beside her. He swung the wide gate closed. "That'll keep him till he settles down." He hugged Abby's shoulders. "Looks like it was a good thing the paddock gate was open, huh, girl?"

Abby blinked and smiled a crooked smile. Then she whimpered, "I almost lost him, and I only just got him."

"Yep," Dad said. "Now you know what can happen."

Mom came up carrying Tuffy. "You wouldn't have lost him, Abby. All he would do is find his way back to the stable, I bet."

Abby thought that over for a second, then she saw Tuffy. "You stupid dog. You almost . . . you almost . . ."

"Don't you yell at Tuffy. You're the one who dropped the rope," said Brad.

"Dropped it? You pulled it away, you . . . you brat!"

"I was trying to help." Brad's lips pouted up.

Dad gave Brad and Abby a level look. "You two got that out of your systems now?" He waited a moment. "Okay, Abby, you and I are going to walk out to the other side of the paddock. And you know what?"

Abby nodded, chewing her lip, then said, "We'll get Griffin."

"Right," he said. "Let's go."

Abby's dad grew vegetables for big grocery stores. So there were several fields on their farm with broccoli, squash, cabbage, lettuce, and sweet corn. But this one fenced field, the paddock, was all grass and clover. Grazing food that horses loved.

It had never seemed so large to Abby before. Sure, Griffin had run as far as he could. Horses are all about saving their own hides, she thought.

Abby's palms felt sweaty as she walked beside Dad. How could I have let go of that rope? she wondered. She'd led horses at Blue Ribbon dozens of times. Maybe hundreds. At least Mr. Winkler didn't see. He would have turned his trailer around and hauled Griffin back to the stable. Her stomach clenched at the thought.

Dad said, "He looks happy as a clam now, doesn't he?" They were still several yards away from Griffin.

"Uh-huh," Abby said, though she was sure she'd never seen a happy clam. "Let's go slow so he doesn't startle."

As they came closer Griffin raised his head to look at them. Then he went back to cropping grass.

"Hey, boy," Abby said. She tried to sound friendly and not anxious. Could she fool him?

Yep. Griffin kept chomping. Slowly he moved a couple steps farther from her. He was smart enough to know why Abby was there, and didn't want to give up a good patch of clover.

Abby and Dad moved with him. She looked at Dad, a question in her eyes. She hated to grab the lead rope. What if . . .

Dad nodded his head yes and folded his arms.

Okay. Guess he expected her to do this. But when she went for the rope, Griffin took two more big steps. "Ohh!" she said. As she closed in on him again, off he moved. No rush, just easing out of her reach. "Come here, you!" How could Griffin treat her like this? He was making her feel like an idiot. Plus, she was beginning to think her legs weren't long enough after all.

"What are you going to do, Abby?" Dad asked. "Play tag all day?"

Tag? This was more like playing Keep Away, and she was losing.

Then she remembered—a horse cookie! She had one in her pants pocket. She had meant to feed it to Griffin when he got off the trailer, then everything went crazy.

She palmed the cookie and hustled out ahead of the horse, not trying to get near the lead rope. She turned and held out her arm, the cookie in her outstretched palm. "Here, Griffin. Come on, boy."

Griffin looked. He snuffed. Then he went to Abby, reached out, and lipped the treat from her. When he did, Abby grabbed his halter, then the lead rope. She swung Griffin around, back to Dad. "He likes horse cookies," she said, grinning.

"Lucky you had one on you," Dad said. "Bring him in, Abby." He started back across the field.

Dad trusted her. That felt good.

She gave a decisive tug, and Griffin plodded along beside her. This was more like it—her horse doing what she wanted him to do. Abby began to relax.

At the gate she said, "I wasn't sure he'd go for it—he really loves our grass."

Dad said, "Oh yeah. Here, he won't have to share with all those lesson horses."

"I'll have to be careful not to give him too much grain," Abby said. "Don't want him tubby, like Marshmallow."

"Hey, don't dis my old buddy." Dad grinned.

"Anyway," Abby added, "Mom and I already have it figured out. How much he should eat because of his weight, his age, and his activity, you know."

"Yep, I've heard you two making plans. Your mother likes things buttoned down tight."

Mom and Brad had waited for their return. Brad charged right into the barn with them.

Abby halted at Marshmallow's stall, where the pony reached his white head over the top board. "Griffin, say hello to Marshmallow."

The horse and pony touched noses.

"They're going to be friends, aren't they?" Brad asked.

"Oh yeah, they are," Abby said. "Besides food, horses love other horses."

"Wonder who's going to be boss," said Mom.

Brad said loudly, "Abby is."

Mom chuckled. But Abby was thinking, Yeah, boss, me. Who else?

"Two horses or ten, one is always boss," Dad said.

"Oh." Abby hadn't remembered that. "Then

Griffin, of course. Look how much bigger he is than Marshmallow."

"I wouldn't be so sure," said Mom.

"Yeah," said Brad. "Bigger isn't always better."

Abby rolled her eyes. "Anyway, I have to show Griffin I'm the boss of him."

Dad said, "Right. Otherwise you're in for real trouble."

Chapter 5

Where Is Devon?

bby led Griffin into his stall. She couldn't stop smiling. "Doesn't he look great in here?" she asked. "All my life I've wanted a horse. Now I've got him."

Dad chuckled. "And not a moment too soon," he said. "Are those gray hairs I see on your head?"

Abby laughed. "Hey, it was a long, long time, okay?"

Dad gave the horse a pat as he turned to leave. "Well, he's had enough excitement for one day. And I've got to get back to work."

Griffin sucked long and deep from his bucket. Abby watched him as if she'd never seen a horse drink before.

"Why don't you come out now and let him get used to the place," Mom suggested.

"Oh, please, pleease! Can't I brush him

some?" Abby already had her brand-new curry-comb in one hand.

"All right. A little." Mom petted the dog which she still held. "Don't forget, even for a minute, Abby, what we talked about."

"I know. I won't forget—be careful in here."

Brad begged, "Can't I be in the stall, too?"

Abby scowled. "You go brush Marshmallow. He'll get jealous."

Brad screwed up his mouth.

Mom said, "I'll take Tuffy to the house with me. Griffin won't bolt every time he hears a dog bark, will he?"

Brad said, "The stable dogs bark sometimes, I guess."

Abby was lost in her own dreamworld, grooming her own horse. She hummed as she worked.

"You would think. Well, I hope he gets used to Tuffy quickly," Mom said as she left.

Brad hung around. "Can I pet him? Can I ride him? Can I do *some*thing, Abby?"

Abby smiled sweetly at her brother. "You can admire Griffin from out there."

"*Grrr,*" Brad grumbled. He kicked the stall wall. Thunk!

Griffin backed away, almost catching Abby's foot.

"Go!" Abby said. "Before you cause another disaster."

"I didn't . . . ," Brad started. Then he seemed to know Abby wasn't listening, and took off.

Abby brushed and brushed the horse's beautiful brown coat. "You like this, don't you?" Griffin's eyelids were drooping. He was happy in his new stall. Abby could tell. And why wouldn't he be, since it was perfect. That made Abby's heart swell up like a big, warm muffin.

She hugged Griffin's neck. Devon would love how silky and shiny . . . Devon! Holy Moly! She had to come see Griffin. She had to come now!

"Gotta go, boy." Abby dropped her brush—no time to put it away. She pushed open the stall door, gave it a closing shove with her heel, and was off in a run. "Gotta call Devon!" she yelled back at Griffin.

When Abby slammed into the family room, Mom's head jerked up. "What's wrong? What's happened?"

Abby was reaching for the phone on the end table. "Huh? Oh, nothing," she said in a rush. "Everything's great, great, great. Except that Devon was supposed to be here." She started punching in numbers. Abby's eyes sparkled at her mother. "Nothing could be better—as soon as I get to show Devon my horse.

"Humph!" Abby said at the phone. "No answer."

"Maybe Devon's—," Mom started.

"I know—maybe she's on her way over here. Sure, that's it. That's gotta be it," Abby said. "I'll go meet her." She tripped over the ottoman.

"Abby! Careful!" Mom said.

She picked herself up, raced through the kitchen and out the back door.

Abby gave a passing glance to the barn and didn't see Devon's bike there. She kept on running down the drive. At the road, she watched. "She'll be here any minute," she told herself.

And watched. "She should be here by now."

And watched. "Phooey. It doesn't take that long from her house. What's wrong with that girl?" She stamped back to the barn. *She* had gone to Devon's a couple of days back to see the newborn kittens. As soon as Devon called. Even though they turned out to be almost as boring as she'd imagined. That's what she had done.

Halfway to the barn Abby deliberately started skipping. No one was going to spoil her best day ever. Not even a best friend.

She hustled on to Griffin's stall. "What?" She skidded to a halt. The stall door was open.

Hands on her hips, Abby called. "Brat, you can't be in there. Not without me, buster."

When there was no answer, Abby hesitated. "Brad?" she said, and cautiously took the last few steps to where she could see in.

"Phew!" No little brother in a heap under a big horse. Good. "Uhhh!" No horse! Not good. Not good at all!

Both hands covered her mouth when she remembered how quickly she'd left the stall. How she hadn't really fastened the door. Had she? No.

Had she lost Griffin again? Already? This horse was more slippery than a new saddle.

Chapter 6

Munch-Crunch!

What was that sound? Abby stood still in the empty stall, eyes wide so she could hear better. The sound came from the tack and feed room.

Oh boy, she thought, I'm in trouble now.

Abby moved into action. At the end of the aisleway, she found Griffin.

He was one happy fellow—his big mouth buried in the grain bin. The lid was on the floor and Griffin was blissfully chewing sweet feed.

Munch-crunch, munch-crunch! The sound echoed in Abby's head like the crack of a lunge whip.

"Bad, Griffin, bad!" Abby said. But what she really thought was bad, Abby. She knew a horse should have a limited amount of rich grain. Extra over time could make him fat, but a lot of grain at one time could make him sick. Sort of like if Abby ate all of her Halloween candy at once.

Abby felt a bit sick now as she eased into the tack and feed room. It was not large. Not with a full-grown horse standing in it, anyway. Abby had to slip around Griffin's big rear, trying not to trip over a hay bale. She remembered to stay to the side of him and place her hand on his haunch so he'd not be surprised she was back there. Getting kicked would put a damper on her perfect day, which already was unperfect.

Guess this was a time for her to show him who was boss. "No, Griffin!" Abby tugged on his halter, trying to raise his head.

Munch-crunch, munch-crunch! Griffin had only one thought in that big head, and that was eating.

A second pull, using both arms this time, got Griffin's head up. But he swung his body around, almost trapping Abby against the wall.

"Whoooa!" Abby dropped her hold, catching her balance. She wiped away the sweat that had popped up on her forehead. Why did Griffin seem so much bigger here than at the stable? And so much harder—no, she wouldn't think it.

Back into the grain bin went Griffin's nose.

"Now you've done it. Now you've made me mad!" Abby scooted herself around in front of Griffin. She grabbed the halter once more, one hand on each side of the horse's head. "Back," she said firmly. "Back up!"

Griffin was trained to follow commands. And there was real command in Abby's voice. He began backing himself out of the room. Abby still held his halter and guided him.

"What are you doing?" Brad startled her.

"Nothing." How much had he seen? Abby wondered.

Brad smirked. "Were too. Doing something. I saw. You let Griffin eat right out of the grain bin. Why'd you do that?"

Abby recognized the gleam in her brother's eyes. Would he tattle? "I was only trying something," she said. "I won't do it again, so keep quiet about it. Promise?"

Brad shrugged. "You're not supposed to let a horse eat right out of the feed bin. You're not."

Abby said carefully, "You're right."

That seemed to suit Brad, so he left her alone. He carried a small hoe out to the nearest field, where Dad was working.

Once Abby had Griffin in his stall, and had checked and double-checked that the door was firmly latched, she felt the steam fizzle out of her. With just enough energy to get the bin cover on tightly, she plodded to the house.

"Was Devon here?" Mom asked.

"Devon?" Abby shook her head. She'd forgotten all about Devon.

"Well, she'll come later," said Mom.

Abby grunted. She went to her room and flopped onto her bed. It wasn't just that Devon had forgotten to come. It was everything. One more scare from her horse and she would . . . she would—

Mom knocked, then poked her head in. "You okay, honey?"

"Tired," Abby mumbled.

Mom gave her back a pat. "It's been a big day. You rest awhile so you can do Griffin's evening feeding."

Her mother closed the door. Abby groaned. She might never get up. Anyway, it would only be hay tonight for Mister Help-Himself.

Chapter 7

A Horse, Not a Pony

In the morning Abby felt bright as the yellow sun. She was dressed—shorts and T-shirt—but her hair was uncombed, teeth unbrushed. She hummed and jiggled her legs and gobbled her cereal. New day. New horse. Had to get out to him.

"Quiet," Brad grumbled, always slow to fully wake up.

"Sorry." Abby gulped her juice and shoved her chair back.

"I'm glad to see you feeling perky again," Mom told her, smiling.

"Is Dad . . . ?" Abby asked.

"He's already out there."

"He didn't feed Griffin, did he?" This morning she was eager to do the job herself.

Mom shook her head. "He'll do the watering, but I'm pretty sure he expects you to feed your horse, sweety." Again she smiled, knowingly.

"You bet," said Abby. "And I get to ride him in a couple of hours!"

That got Brad's attention. "I want to ride with you. Can I, me and Marshmallow?"

Abby grinned. "Sure. It'll be fun." Riding her own horse at her own home. How great was that? And Marshmallow was going to be totally impressed with Griffin.

The phone rang. Abby pounced. "Devon! Where were you yesterday? Not here, for sure," she rattled.

"I forgot I had my violin lesson," said Devon.

"You could have come over after. I *really* wanted to show you Griffin."

"But then Mom said we'd go see Willa, my cousin. I can come now. Would it be okay?" Devon asked.

"Well . . ." Abby pretended to be thinking about it. "Yes! Get. Over. Here!"

Abby hustled to the barn. Tuffy danced beside her. Dib and Dab quacked and flounced as she slipped between them.

But when she reached the stall, Abby stopped and stood there a minute, her fingers laced beneath her chin. "Hi, Griff," she said on a breath. He was still there. He was still hers. Griffin the gorgeous.

The horse stomped and whinnied. Dad gave

her a tap on the arm. "You know what he's saying, don't you, girl?"

Abby laughed. "Uh-huh. Where's breakfast?"

"Good, you understand Horse," her father said.

"You bet."

"What's your plan?" Dad asked. "I've fed Marshmallow."

Abby said, "I'm going to feed Griffin right now."

"And then?" Dad said.

"Oh, Devon's on her way here. Then I'm showing her my horse." Abby turned her face up at her dad, feeling good.

"Okay. And then?"

Abby frowned. "I'll . . . I know. When he's all through eating and being superadmired, I'll turn him out into the paddock, and then I can muck out his stall." She looked. Yep, just like Devon said, there was poop to clean.

Dad was nodding. "Sounds like a plan all right. I'll be in the toolshed if you need me."

Abby just knew she wouldn't need help. Today she was sure, sure, sure she could take care of her horse. She went for a flake of hay and half a scoop of grain. The grain smelled yummy—better than her own cereal—as she poured it into Griffin's feed bucket. His soft mouth was all over the food almost before she'd emptied the scoop. She loosened the hay and put it in a pile on the floor; Griffin could work at it like he was grazing.

Abby heard Devon before she saw her. She hurried to the big, open barn door.

Devon was saying, "Hi, Dib and Dab, you funny duckies. Why won't you ever let me pet you? Pretty white ducks, big yellow feet. Why?"

Abby frowned. How could Devon be thinking about Dib and Dab now? "Devon, they aren't pets. They're just Dad's token farm animals—at least that's what he calls them—not pets.

"Come on, Devon. Come, come! You have to see." Abby grabbed her friend's hand and pulled her along.

Devon said, "Okay," and had her can't-wait look on.

A few steps farther Abby said, "Hold it, hold it. Close your eyes." She clamped her hand over Devon's eyes to make sure. "Now when you open them, you'll see him all at once."

"All right," Devon said, and let Abby walk her to the stall.

Abby removed her hand from Devon's face.
Silence.

"Devon. Open your eyes," Abby bossed.

"Oh, wow," said Devon. "He's pretty."

"Isn't he? Beautiful, I'd say. You haven't really seen his face." Griffin had his neck lowered to chew on his pile of hay.

The girls leaned against the stall door. "See how perfect his tail is?" Abby said. "And—"

Griffin swept his head up and over the top board, a strand of hay dangling from his teeth.

Devon gulped and stumbled back.

Abby just laughed. "Come here, Devon. It's okay."

Devon crept nearer.

"See," said Abby, "how gorgeous his face is, and his eyes—even his long eyelashes—and his white spot on his forehead, that's called a star, even though it isn't quite shaped like one."

When Abby turned to her, Devon nodded and smiled. "I like his eyes, and . . . and his star," she said. "I was just surprised. He's bigger than Marshmallow. A lot."

"Mm-hmm," Abby said, pleased. "Griffin's a horse. Marshmallow's a pony." Griffin went for another bite of hay, then came back to the girls. "He likes people. Why don't you pat his cheek so he knows you like him?"

Devon reached her hand up. She stroked Griffin's cheek, squinting her eyes as if she didn't know what to expect. "Kind of soft," she said. Then she giggled. "I can feel him chewing!"

Abby grinned. "He's wonderful."

Just then Griffin turned his head quickly and bumped Devon's shoulder. "Oh!" she said, and backed away again. "He sure moves fast."

Tuffy came padding toward the girls, wagging his tail.

Devon squatted down to pet and hug him.

Abby frowned. "Tuffy be good." She told Devon, "Griffin's not sure he likes Tuffy barking."

Devon said, "But a dog's gotta bark."

"Oh yeah? You should have seen yesterday . . . ," she started, but stopped herself. "Well, anyhow, Griffin was just excited getting here yesterday. And Tuffy was all worried by the big noisy trailer and truck. It's not a problem."

Devon raised her eyebrows. "Now I wish I had been here," she said. "Tuffy, Tuffy, were you a naughty boy?" She scratched his ears gently.

"He was," said Abby, "even though I know you don't think so." She shrugged. "Anyway, I got everything back under control."

"I'm glad," Devon said. She stood, and the two of them listened to Griffin rustle hay. And each thought her own thoughts.

Chapter 8

A Big Chicken!

Griffin took a slurp of water, finished with his hay for the time being.

Abby grabbed the lead rope from its nail and unlatched the stall door.

Devon's eyes got big.

"Yeah, exciting, isn't it?" said Abby. "Now you'll see all of him." She swung open the door, hooked the lead to Griffin's halter. Abby was almost humming. This felt so easy today. So different from the day before. She walked the horse into the aisle and past Devon.

Devon stayed plastered to the wall.

"Come on," Abby said. "We're going to the paddock. Come on."

Griffin's slow steps clunked the cement as Abby guided him ahead.

Devon started walking, carefully.

"Not behind him," Abby fussed. "Alongside him, like me."

Devon said, "Well, maybe I don't want to be that close."

Abby stopped. "Huh? Come here. I'll teach you how to lead."

"I'm not going to walk that big thing," Devon said, shaking her head.

"Oh, Dev. Don't be such a noodle." What was the matter with Devon? Griffin wasn't about to hurt her. Griffin was great. Why couldn't she just try to . . . "You know"—Abby set a hand on her hip—"I went right over to your house when the kittens were born to see them. It's your turn now. And they were about as fun as watching ice melt in Siberia."

Devon huffed. "You said they were cute. You said they were adorable."

Abby shrugged and patted Griffin, who was getting impatient.

"Well, crumb, Abby—" Devon glared at her. "You lied! You lied to me," she cried.

"I wanted to make you feel good. That's what friends are for, you know." She didn't like being called a liar. She didn't like anything that was happening.

"Friends are for . . . ," Devon spat out. "Friends are supposed to understand!" She ran outside and hopped onto her bike.

"Devon! Don't!" Abby shouted.

Devon turned her head to answer. "And the kitties *are* adorable."

"Ohhh! I *do* understand," Abby yelled after her. "You're a big chicken!"

Abby stood watching her friend pedal away, blond hair flying. She couldn't believe what Devon had said. She couldn't believe what *she* had said.

Griffin shuffled his feet. He pushed his chin forward, asking to go.

"Okay, boy. Sorry," Abby muttered. She got him out and into the paddock and shut the gate.

Griffin took off trotting. Then he kicked up his heels and galloped. Whee, he was happy to be free!

Abby's eyes followed his every move. He was so full of energy. So strong. So graceful. How she'd wanted Devon to love him.

"Pooh! Some best friend!" she said, and kicked a fence post. She stomped back to the stall.

With a pitchfork Abby scooped up droppings and flung them into the wheelbarrow. It felt better to be doing something. Turning the shavings with her fork, she picked out the wet spot. This was one mighty big bathroom, she thought.

As she rolled the barrow to the manure pile in back of the barn, she finally stopped frowning over the argument. Abby felt great that she had been able to make Griffin's home nice and neat again. She did it. All herself.

Chapter 9

The Best Ride

"Hurry up, Brad. Get your boots on. If you're riding with Griffin and me, you can't be pokey." Abby was in jeans and her paddock boots. She checked the hall mirror as she buckled her helmet strap. Ready to roll, she thought. She took a deep breath.

"I'll beat ya there," Brad said, sliding around her and out the front door.

"Oh, you!" Abby ran, but she didn't care if he got to the barn first. She was going to be *so* ahead of him on Griffin. Dib and Dab quacked hello as she scooted by them.

Dad was hooking up a wagon to his John Deere utility tractor in the barnyard. He followed the two into the barn as soon as he finished.

Abby had Griffin fastened on his cross ties in the aisle. She was already giving him a quick brushing to get his hair all comfy before being tacked. Brad was doing the same for Marshmallow.

She was so eager to be riding, Abby almost forgot to pick out Griffin's hooves. Would have forgotten if she hadn't seen Brad working on Marshmallow's.

She carefully lifted one hoof after another. Each time, she gave a quick cleaning to be sure nothing was packed in that could hurt Griffin, then stowed the hoof pick.

It seemed crazy to Abby, the way her heart was thumping as she placed the saddle pad on Griffin's back. After all, she'd done this lots of times at the stable.

But this was *here*. This was home and all new.

"Good thing you've been keeping this old saddle and bridle clean and oiled," Dad said, handing the small English saddle to her.

Abby nodded. Oh, yeah, she'd known she would have her own horse one day. Dad watched to be sure she could reach high enough to put the saddle into place, and checked to see it was far enough forward, but not too far.

Abby grabbed the girth and fastened it around Griffin's belly. Then Griffin lowered his head enough to make it easy to get the bridle with reins and bit on him; he'd learned a lot by being a lesson horse.

Brad grunted as he hoisted a saddle onto Marshmallow. Abby usually helped, but this time Dad did. Anyway, her brother was nearly big enough to do the tacking himself.

With another deep breath Abby led Griffin to the mounting block. At last, she was on her horse! She thought she should get a gold star for patience—he'd been here almost a full day already.

Yep! Home looked different from up there—different from what it had on little Marshmallow. Felt different from being in the ring at the stable. As she touched her heels to Griffin's side Abby knew she was smiling a barn-size smile.

Dad stood at the paddock fence. "What's your choice, Abby?"

She'd thought a lot about this first ride. A lot, a lot. "It might be good to be in a fenced-in place, since that's what Griffin's used to. But I think he already knows the paddock is where he goes to play. And eat. I might never keep him moving. And I don't think going on the trails—"

"What's wrong with the trails?" Brad butted in. "The trails are good."

Dad was watching Abby.

She tightened the girth one more notch now that she was on the horse. "I want to walk and trot around the outside of this fence. That might help Griffin feel calm, I think."

Brad made a face.

Abby said, "Then if he's being good, we could do some cantering over there where it's open, but not a field where the footing might be rough, and not in the woods."

Dad gave a thumbs-up.

Another touch of her heels and they were on their way. Abby could tell Griffin was happy to be out for a ride, same as she was. His ears were perked forward. She could feel him taking the bit and going willingly.

They walked slowly at first, Marshmallow and Brad following. Griffin's warm smell and the rhythm of his movement beneath her seemed so good to Abby.

To her surprise Marshmallow pulled ahead of Griffin. "Brat," Abby muttered. It felt too great to be riding for her to really mind, though. A light summer breeze was blowing, the sky was perfect, perfect blue, and Abby was on her own horse. Perfect, perfect! Well, except for Devon not being here to watch and see how good she looked up on Griffin. How awesome her horse looked when he was ridden.

Soon Abby asked for a trot. She passed Brad. It was either that or run into Marshmallow's rear.

"Hey!" said Brad. "We wanted to lead."

Abby looked back. "Griffin's covering ground

faster than Marshmallow. Face it, his legs are a lot longer."

Marshmallow was trotting too now. Brad yelled, "I want to lead. Or else I'll tell Dad what you did yesterday."

Abby stopped. She waited until Brad was beside her. "What? What did I do yesterday?"

Brad said, "You know."

Abby clenched her jaw. She didn't like making mistakes. She would like even less for Dad to know that she'd let Griffin escape his stall and get into the sweet feed. "Okay," she agreed reluctantly. "Get going." She would give them a good head start, then canter a ways.

This was supposed to be fun, more fun than anything. And so it would be. Brad couldn't ruin this ride. She wouldn't let him. And at least *he* liked Griffin. She wished he would grow up, though. She almost laughed out loud when Griffin took off at her signal. She loved his smoothness; she loved the muffled sound of his hooves on the grass. She was flying.

She did pass Brad and Marshmallow once again. She had to. But then she halted and turned to watch them catch up and go on ahead.

Silly little brother, she thought. It was good, though, to be the big one. And up on Griffin she really *was* big.

Chapter 10

Alone on the Trail

bby sank into bed that night with stars in her eyes. She would sleep well after her huge, first full day with Griffin. She knew any dreams she might have couldn't measure up to her wonderful real life.

In the morning Abby stretched like a cat, smiling. Yesterday—what fun. She had fed Griffin and made him happy. She had turned him out to run and graze and made him happy. She had cleaned his stall about as clean as could be. She'd brushed him shiny, and best of all had ridden him very nicely—walk, trot, canter, walk again to cool off—and made *herself* happy (she thought Griffin loved it too, though). Then she'd fed him once more and kissed his nose good night.

Even if Devon didn't get it, having Griffin was the best thing ever.

For Abby the most special part of each day was riding her horse. That was her reward for all the jobs that went with having Griffin. That and having him as her new best friend.

She took time one day to get Tuffy and Griffin better acquainted. Fearless Tuffy liked being around horses. And Griffin didn't seem bothered having him in the barn. But Abby wondered what he would do if Tuffy got too excited again. As a test, she ran up and down the aisle with Tuffy. Of course, Tuffy yapped and yapped. Griffin put his head out to watch the craziness. Abby thought he was smiling, not upset at all. Boy, Devon should have seen that. She'd have laughed.

Abby took her weekly lesson at the stable one day. It wasn't as much fun now that she had her own horse. But she had to keep on learning so maybe someday she could be in a horse show with Griffin.

Usually in summers Abby and Devon saw each other nearly every day. Abby was almost, *almost* too busy to miss that.

By the fourth day Brad didn't want to ride with Abby. "Mom said I can go to Stewie's house to swim. It's hot. It'll be fun."

Swimming did sound like fun, Abby thought. And she liked Stewie's sister, Lynne. Could she go, too? she wondered.

As if he read her mind, Brad said, "Lynne is

gone somewhere, so it's just me and him and his two cousins. You wouldn't like it."

Rats! Abby hadn't been swimming much at all this summer. All that nice cool water, the splashing, the screeching. Usually she and Devon . . . She shrugged. "You can still go riding with me. We don't have to wait till afternoon."

"Nah. Who wants to ride every day?" he answered.

Mom had come into the kitchen. "You and Devon should plan something," she told Abby. "I haven't seen her since you got Griffin."

"She was here. She met Griffin."

"Yeah," said Brad, "they had a big fight."

"Don't you ever mind your own business?" Abby fumed.

"What?" said Mom. "Who did? Griffin and Devon?"

Brad giggled. "No, Abby and Devon."

"You be quiet!" Abby said. Then she dropped her chin and bit back tears.

Mom took her by the shoulders. "Honey. I didn't know. What happened?"

Abby wailed, "She hates my horse!"

"Oh, surely not," Mom said.

"Yes. Yes, she does!" Abby hadn't wanted to talk about their argument. But, of course, Brad had to blab. She shot a burning look his way.

"Give her some time," Mom was saying. "She'll come around. You two have been best friends for a long—"

Abby pulled away. "I've got to get out to the barn." She didn't want to be reminded of how long she and Devon had been best friends. Didn't want to think about how much she was missing Devon.

Abby decided to ride early. It would be better than in the heat of the afternoon. And besides, Brad was still home and might change his mind about riding when he saw her getting ready.

Sure enough, as she finished tacking Griffin, Abby heard the scuffle of Brad's feet. She couldn't help grinning, but kept at her work.

"You know, I might ride," Brad started.

"That's okay. You don't have to," Abby said. She wasn't going to make it easy for him.

"But I will, Abby. If I can ride Griffin."

"Brad, what are you thinking? You ride Marshmallow. You're not ready for Griffin yet."

Brad fidgeted a minute. Then he said, "If you don't let me, I'll tell Dad what you did."

Abby huffed. "What now?"

"About how you let Griffin get loose, and he got into the tack room—"

"Give it up, brat. I told Dad myself two days ago."

"Huh?"

"You heard me. I told him."

"Oh . . . Are you in trouble?"

"No." She looked right at him. "He said we could mark it up to being all nervous about Griffin's first day here. And that he liked what he was seeing, the way I've been taking care of everything. So we'd forget about that."

Brad said, "Oh-kay. I still want to ride Griffin." He smiled as if he'd said something clever.

Abby walked the horse to the mounting block. "Maybe when you stop being a tattletale. Maybe then."

Brad wrinkled his lips. Then he ran off, calling for Tuffy.

Abby thought she would go on a trail ride. Yesterday she and Brad had been on the trails, and Griffin was happy and good.

She started Griffin at a walk, then trotted when they got to the shade of the woods. The trail wound through tall oak trees, maples, and honey locust. Cooler and airy, not too closed in. "I like this, Griff, just you and me," she said, patting his shoulder. Abby felt free and in her own world. She could hear cardinals calling each other, feel the air kissing her cheeks. Brad may not want to, but she could do this every day. With so much practice she would get to be—"Ohhh!"

Griffin had slammed on his brakes and thrown up his head. Abby was tossed forward, her chest hitting his neck. One hand grabbed for the mane, something to hold on to. She felt a foot slide from its stirrup, and she gripped the reins hard with her other hand.

Yipes, Abby thought, he almost dumped me!

A white-tailed deer had leaped across the trail and crashed back through the trees. Now Griffin stood blowing, his nostrils working, rib cage bellowing in and out. Abby could feel the thump of his heartbeat through her leg.

She straightened herself up and found the stirrup with her toe. She hadn't heard that deer, hadn't seen it until it was too late. "It's okay, boy." She calmed the horse once she got herself settled. She stroked his shoulder and got him to turn back the way they had come.

Everything *was* okay, but her stomach felt full of marbles. What would she do if she got thrown while riding by herself?

Her head seemed light from the aftershock, but she thought and thought as Griffin walked. Maybe Dad and Mom trusted me a little too much. Maybe I don't deserve to be out riding whenever I feel like it.

No, she would make things work. She should practice getting on Griffin from the ground

instead of the mounting block. Yeah, that would be a good idea. In fact, she'd have to think twice about riding alone away from the house.

After a few days Abby had taught herself how to get in the saddle without the mounting block or a leg up. Still, if she got thrown, she might be hurt. Or . . . well, she still might have to walk the horse home. She mulled that over as she lingered in bed rubbing her tired eyes. Her whole body was tired. Taking care of Griffin—huh!

It was hard.

She loved it.

It was hard.

She hated it.

It was hard.

She loved Griffin!

So it wasn't *too* hard. She crawled out of bed, ready to do it all over again.

Chapter 11

Missing Devon

Two weeks, Abby thought as she pulled on her clothes. I've had Griffin now for two weeks. Oof, she had some sore muscles to prove it. Slowly she made her way to the kitchen and found the family already gathered there.

"Abby girl!" Dad greeted her from the stove, where he was scrambling eggs. "You look like you could use some grub."

Abby faked a smile and flopped into her chair.

Mom patted her. "Let's go shopping today. Make a day of it. You need a couple pairs of new shorts. And you're outgrowing those sandals you keep wearing."

Abby brightened. "Maybe I can get some just like them. Can we have lunch at Burger Guy? Oh, but wait, I have Griffin to—"

Dad set a plate with eggs and a buttered English muffin before Abby. "Time for a break.

You're going to bust your git-along if you don't ease up, girly."

"Da-ad. Stop talking like an old cowboy," Brad said.

"Why, durn my hide, I never!" said Dad.

"Dad's right," Mom said. "In spite of his weirdness. You've proven beyond doubt that you can take care of your horse. But you don't have to give up everything else."

Abby blinked. But she kind of did, didn't she?

"I don't mind feeding Griffin some mornings, Abby," Dad said as he sat down to eat with them. "And you don't have to ride every single day. Even Griffin would like a rest, I guess."

Should she? Shouldn't she? When school started, she wouldn't be able to spend nearly as much time with her horse. But she sure was missing all the other summer things she liked to do. She sure was missing having a friend to do them with.

Oh, what was her problem? It wouldn't kill Griffin not to see her for a few hours. Besides, Dad was going to help out. A day's break from riding might keep her from feeling like a worn-out old cowgirl herself.

So Abby and her mother drove to the mall and had a good time. When they got back home late that afternoon, Abby loved seeing her horse out in the paddock. He was happy doing his thing. She'd been happy doing hers. And tonight she could feed him without resenting it.

At day's end Brad and Abby ran around outside chasing fireflies. It was magical. It made her laugh right out loud at how pretty the dark air was with all the blinking little lights. She would ask Devon if she liked lightning bugs. She bet she did. They were small. They were pretty. They wouldn't hurt you. Tomorrow . . . tomorrow she was going to phone Devon.

But the next day turned gray and rainy. Abby's mood went downhill with the weather. Why couldn't Devon call *her*? Or ride her bike over, like she used to all the time? Huh? I'm not the one who ran off all crazy mad for no good reason, Abby thought.

When she got to the barn, Griffin's welcome nicker cheered her—at least a bit. "Hi, boy. Come here."

He stuck his head over the stall door and let her rub his face. He could smell the carrot she had, though, and poked his nose around her pocket.

"Wait, wait. Don't be so grabby." She held the carrot in her palm for Griffin to take. She half smiled listening to him crunch and slobber over the treat.

Looked like she wouldn't be riding again, because of the weather. So it would be a good day to clean her saddle.

Abby got the little red wagon she and Brad used to play with—well, Brad still did—loaded her saddle into it, and pulled it to the house. She wanted someday to learn how to use a Western saddle too, but for now she was glad she only had this smaller saddle to handle.

In the laundry room, off the kitchen, she rubbed special saddle soap on the leather.

Mom came to start a load of wash. She said, "You look kind of like a rain cloud yourself, Abby."

"Mmff," Abby answered.

"Did you know the county fair is next week?"

Abby glanced up, afraid to say anything. The fair had been super last year. She and Devon had seen all the fancy chickens and rabbits and ridden nearly every ride. Devon had even given Abby her last token so she could try to win a goldfish.

"I'd be glad to take you and Devon. You'll have fun."

"Yeah, but . . ." Abby squirmed.

Mom said, "I know you two are still on the outs. But maybe it's time to get past that. What do you think?"

"I want to, Mom. I can't."

"Can't, or won't?" Mom asked.

"Devon's a scaredy-cat! Cats! She likes cats better than horses."

Mom twisted the knob on the washer. "That's nothing new, is it? She's still the same girl she was before you got Griffin."

Abby scrubbed harder, her eyebrows drawn down. Finally she said, "I thought she'd see how wonderful Griffin is. He's *my* horse, and if she's my friend, she has to like him a little."

Mom nodded. "Maybe you could help her to feel more comfortable around him. I doubt she likes being afraid of him."

Abby wouldn't meet her mother's eyes. But she said, "Yeah. I think . . . I bet I could."

Chapter 12

A Little Bit at a Time

Abby punched in the number that she knew better than anybody's. She wondered if Devon would answer when she read who was calling her.

But then Abby heard that familiar voice. "Hi, Devon, it's me," she said. She tried to sound like this call was nothing unusual, but her insides were jumping.

"Hi," was all Devon would say.

Abby blurted the first thing she could think of. "Do the kitties have their eyes open yet?"

Devon laughed. "Sure. They've been open for a long time. You'd be surprised how much they've changed since . . . well, you know . . . since the one time you came to see them."

Abby thought that meant she was supposed to apologize. Not what she'd had in mind. Still, it couldn't hurt. "I'm sorry I haven't been over. But you're mad at me, remember?"

"You're mad at me, too," Devon said.

"Not anymore. I don't want to be," said Abby.

"Me neither."

"Can I maybe come over now? To see you . . . and the kittens?"

Fifteen minutes later Abby was at Devon's house.

"You don't have to look at the kittens," Devon said. "We can just stay outside."

Abby said, "I really want to. You like them a lot, so it's fine. They're just not as exciting to me as a horse is."

"I know," said Devon. "Or as scary."

Abby wanted to shout, Horses aren't scary once you know them, but she kept quiet. Even more, she wanted to understand her friend.

"Wow, they've sure grown," she said when she and Devon crouched near the kitties' box.

Three bundles of fur were sleeping curled up. Another was yawning, and Abby couldn't help laughing at his big pink mouth and little pink tongue. "Now that's a yawn!" she said.

A fifth kitten had its tiny paws clamped over the side of the box, trying to pull its way out. "Oops, here comes Cleo," said Devon. The yellow kitten dropped onto the floor, looking pleased with herself.

Abby grinned. "Guess she's the escape artist."

"All of them can climb out now," Devon told her. "They won't be in their box much longer."

Cleo skittered across the floor. Devon reached for her and cuddled her close. "Listen, you can hear her purring."

"Can I pet her?"

Devon said, "Sure. Or get another one out. They're all waking up now we're here. You might like that one in the corner—see, the one that has a white spot on his face. Isn't he cute?"

"Oh my gosh," Abby said, reaching for the kitten. "Almost like Griffin with his white star." She held the kitty in her lap, stroking it softly. She felt his purr buzzing like a motor, and then he licked her with a sandpaper tongue. "Only your eyes are gold," she told him, "and Griffin's are almost black, and your fur is gray and Griffin's is brown."

"Yeah, almost exactly not at all the same," Devon said, and both girls laughed.

It felt good, so good, Abby thought. Nothing was quite the same as laughing with her old best friend.

Jezebel stepped into the box and stretched out to feed her litter. The girls quickly returned Cleo and the white-faced kitten to her.

As they walked back outside Abby said, "Mom says the county fair is next week." She looked at Devon hopefully.

Devon took in a breath. Her eyes sparkled.

"Would you go with me?" Abby dared to ask.

Devon twined her arm in Abby's. "Yes! Oh, we'll have so much fun."

"It will be perfect, perfect, perfect," said Abby. Oh, why had she waited so long to make up with Devon? It had just been confusing, loving Griffin so much and having Devon *not* love him. Now she could see that she and Devon were as different as they were alike in lots of ways, and that was okay.

Then Devon surprised Abby. "Now it's my turn to see Griffin again. He *is* beautiful, Abby, he is. He's just, you know—"

"I know. Come on. Let's go! I promise not to make you get close to him. Not yet, maybe not ever."

"I do like Marshmallow. So maybe I will get so that Griffin doesn't scare me. Maybe not till I'm bigger. I don't know."

"Get on that bike. Let's go, go, go, girl. I'm going to help you get to know my horse a little bit at a time."